Karen's Baby

**Look for these
and other books about Karen
in the
Baby-sitters Little Sister series:**

Little Sister

Karen's Baby

Ann M. Martin

Illustrations by Susan Tang

AN
APPLE
PAPERBACK

SCHOLASTIC INC.
New York Toronto London Auckland Sydney

For Eddie Peterson,
the Cat Man of Park Slope

Activities by Nancy E. Krulik
Activity illustrations by Heather Saunders

No part of this publication may be reproduced in whole or in part, or stored in a retrieval system, or transmitted in any form or by any means, electronic, mechanical, photocopying, recording, or otherwise, without written permission of the publisher. For information regarding permission, write to Scholastic Inc., 730 Broadway, New York, NY 10003.

ISBN 0-590-45649-0

12 11 10 9   /9

Printed in the U.S.A.   40

First Scholastic printing, December 1992

Rachael or Joseph

Here is what I want more than anything in the world. A baby sister or brother. I am not picky. Either one will do.

"Mommy? You know what I would name a baby?" I said. "I would name it Rachael or Joseph."

"I thought you would name it Susan or Tony," said Andrew. Andrew is my little brother. He is four going on five. *I* am seven. And I know that sometimes people change their minds. I had changed my mind a lot about names for a baby. But

Rachael and Joseph were my final choices. I was not going to change my mind again.

"Rachael and Joseph are very nice names," replied Mommy.

"Thank you," I said.

It was a Friday afternoon. I was in the kitchen at the little house with Mommy and Andrew. I am Karen Brewer. I am in second grade. I wear glasses, and I have blonde hair and blue eyes and some freckles.

My mommy and daddy are divorced. They live in two houses now, the little house and the big house. Besides Andrew, I have stepbrothers and a stepsister and an adopted sister. But no *baby* brother or sister.

"Mommy, could you please have a baby?" I asked.

"Karen, we have talked about this before," said Mommy. "It is out of the question. No babies. Besides, you have a little brother."

"But Andrew is not a baby."

"Yeah," agreed Andrew. "I am not a baby."

"Nancy gets to have a baby," I pointed out.

"That is her parents' decision," said Mommy.

Nancy Dawes is one of my two best friends. She is seven, like me. And soon she would be a big sister. Her mother was going to have a baby at any moment. And Nancy would get to name the baby. It was a very exciting time.

The doorbell rang then. I ran to answer it. Guess who had come over. Nancy Dawes. She lives right next door.

"Hi! Is your mother having the baby? Is it coming?" I asked.

"Not yet," said Nancy. She stepped inside.

"Boo," I said.

"Well, it will come when it wants to," said Nancy. "Babies do things when the time is right, you know."

Nancy and I went to the kitchen.

"Hi, honey," said Mommy to Nancy. "How is your mother feeling?"

"She's fine. She went to the doctor today."

"Is she sick? Is the baby sick?" I cried.

"Oh, no. She just has to have lots of checkups, that's all. That is what happens when the baby is almost ready to be born."

I thought Nancy seemed awfully calm for someone who was about to become a big sister. *I* was more nervous than she was. Her mother could start to have the baby at *any second*. That was why I had been calling Mrs. Dawes on the phone so often.

I decided it was time to call her again.

"But I just came from my house," Nancy reminded me. "Mommy is not having the baby yet. She is reading a book."

"The baby has to start coming *some*time," I replied. I dialed the phone. "Hello, Mrs. Dawes? Hi, it's me, Karen. . . . What? . . . It isn't? How did you know I was going to ask? . . . Oh, okay. Okay, 'bye." I hung

4

up. "The baby is not coming yet," I said. "Boy, Nancy. You are the luckiest person alive."

"Well," said Nancy. "I do not think I could be lucky and dead."

No More Babies

Nancy seemed calm about the baby, but I think she was excited inside. She was just trying to act grown-up. A new baby is a big deal, and Nancy knows it. Everybody knows it. That is why I wanted a baby brother or sister of my own so badly.

Just before dinner that night, Mommy drove Andrew and me over to Daddy's house, the big house. We were going to spend the weekend there. Andrew and I have two families and two houses. This is how that happened. A long time ago, when I was a little kid, I lived in the big house with Mommy and Daddy and my brother. But then Mommy and Daddy got divorced. They decided they did not love each other anymore. And they did not want to live together. So Mommy moved out. She took Andrew and me with her. (Daddy stayed behind in the big house. He had grown up there.) Mommy moved us into the little house. After awhile, she and Daddy got married again. But not to each other. Mommy married Seth. He is my stepfather. Daddy married Elizabeth. She is my stepmother.

These are the people in my little-house family: Mommy, Seth, Andrew, me. These are the pets at the little house: Rocky, Midgie, Emily Junior. Rocky and Midgie are Seth's cat and dog. Emily Junior is my rat.

These are the people in my big-house family: Daddy, Elizabeth, Kristy, Charlie, Sam, David Michael, Emily Michelle, Nannie, Andrew, me. These are the pets at the big house: Shannon, Boo-Boo, Goldfishie, Crystal Light the Second. (It is a good thing the big house is a big house.) Kristy, Sam, Charlie, and David Michael are Elizabeth's kids, so they are my stepsister and stepbrothers. Kristy is thirteen and I adore her. She baby-sits. Charlie and Sam go to high school. David Michael is seven like me, but he does not go to my school. Emily is my adopted sister. (I named my rat after her.) She is two and a half. Daddy and Elizabeth adopted her from a faraway country called Vietnam. Emily does not talk much, but Daddy says look out, she will someday. Nannie is Elizabeth's mother. She feels like another grandmother to me. Nannie helps take care of all us kids. Shannon is David Michael's puppy, and Boo-Boo is Daddy's fat old tomcat. Guess what Goldfishie and Crystal Light the Second are. Goldfish. (Duh.) They belong to Andrew and me.

By the way, I have a special nickname

for my brother and me. I call us Andrew Two-Two and Karen Two-Two. (I thought of those names after my teacher read a book to my class. The book was called *Jacob Two-Two Meets the Hooded Fang*.) We are two-twos because we have two families and two houses, two mommies and two daddies, two cats and two dogs, and two of lots of other things. I even have two best friends. They are Hannie Papadakis and Nancy. Hannie lives across the street from Daddy. (And Nancy lives next door to Mommy. Remember?) Hannie and Nancy and I call ourselves the Three Musketeers. We do lots of things together. We are even in the same class at school. Ms. Colman is our teacher. We love her.

Most of the time, I like being a two-two. Now was one of those times. Mommy said she and Seth were not going to have a baby.

But I had one more chance. I could ask Elizabeth to have a baby. Sometimes having two mothers comes in handy.

Guess what Elizabeth said.

No.

She said, "I'm sorry, honey. Your father and I do not plan to have a baby. No more babies. We have enough children."

Baby Presents

The next day was Saturday. As soon as I had eaten breakfast, Hannie came over. We like to get an early start on the day. (Sam saw Hannie and said, "Is she here al*ready*?" But we ignored him.)

Since the weather was very cold and windy, Hannie and I decided to play in my room. We also decided to invite Nancy over for the day.

"I have to call her house anyway," I said. "I have to find out if the baby is here yet."

Hannie and I called Nancy from the

kitchen. Mrs. Dawes answered the phone.

"Hi," I said. "It's me, Karen. . . . It isn't? Darn. Well, may I speak to Nancy, please?"

An hour later, Hannie and Nancy and I were sitting on my bed. We were trying to think of something to do.

"I know!" I cried. "Let's make presents for Nancy's baby."

"Yeah!" exclaimed Hannie.

"But remember," said Nancy. "We will have to give them to the baby *after* he is born. Or she," she added.

"I know. No baby things in your house until the baby has arrived safe and sound," I said. "That is okay. If we wait we can give our presents to the baby in person. Anyway, it will probably take a long time to *make* presents."

"What could we make?" asked Hannie.

"Oh, lots of things," I told her. "We could make a mobile, or a picture to hang on the wall, or an alphabet book, or a decoration for the room."

"Cool! Let's find your stuff," said Nancy.

12

Nancy meant our art materials. In both of my houses are boxes full of scraps of material, balls of yarn, tubes of glitter, stickers, crayons, paints, scissors, glue, old magazines, and more. We are allowed to use the materials to make whatever we want. We just have to be sure to work on newspapers and to clean up our messes.

My friends and I moved into the playroom. We looked at the supplies.

"I am going to make a mobile," said Hannie. "To hang over the crib."

"I am going to make pictures of Mommy and Daddy and me," said Nancy. "We can put them on the wall. That way the baby will know everyone in his family. Or her family."

"What are you going to make, Karen?" asked Hannie.

"I have not decided yet. There are so many things. Let me see. I could knit something for the baby. A hat, maybe. Or a sweater. I know how to knit."

"Could you really knit a sweater?" asked Nancy.

"Well, no," I admitted. "But maybe I could knit a blanket. I made a scarf once. A blanket would just be like a bigger scarf."

Hannie and Nancy and I got to work. Hannie cut out squares of cardboard. She began to color designs on them. Nancy drew a picture of her mother. She drew it carefully. She used a pencil. (She erased a lot.)

I found a pair of knitting needles and some red yarn. It took forever to knit one row. It took forever to knit the next row, too. By then, Hannie's mobile was half finished. Nancy had begun drawing her father.

"The baby will be ten years old by the time this blanket is done!" I exclaimed. "I better make something else."

I found some felt. I found some more yarn. I cut out pieces of felt and sewed them together. "Hey! This pouch is the perfect size to hold a bottle!" I said. "This could

be a bottle-warmer." After I made the bottle-warmer, I made a felt hat.

After the felt hat, I was tired of making presents. So were Hannie and Nancy.

We put the art supplies away. We cleaned up our mess. Then I telephoned Mrs. Dawes. "Is the baby here yet?" I asked.

It wasn't.

The Baby-sitters Club

Nancy and Hannie and I did not know what to do with ourselves. We were not exactly bored, but . . .

"Kristy?" I said. Kristy was in her room. She was stretched out on her bed. She was reading a book. I think she was doing homework.

"Yes?" Kristy looked up. Nancy and Hannie and I were standing in her doorway. "What are you guys doing?" she asked.

"We aren't sure," I said. "What are you doing?"

"My homework. I want to finish it early. I am having a sleepover tonight."

"You are? Where?"

"Here. My friends in the Baby-sitters Club are coming over."

"Cool!" I cried. And then I got a great idea.

I asked Daddy and Elizabeth if I could have a sleepover of my own. Maybe the Three Musketeers could have a party that night, too.

"I suppose so," said Daddy.

"We might as well get everything over with at once," said Elizabeth.

That night the big house was bursting with people. Everyone was at home. Then the guests came. Hannie, Nancy, and Kristy's friends — Mary Anne, Dawn, Stacey, Claudia, Mal, Jessi, and Shannon. (Shannon the person, not Shannon the dog.)

"Karen," said Daddy to my friends and

me, "promise you will leave the big girls alone. Please do not pester them."

We promised.

But guess what. The big girls let us come into Kristy's room. They were putting on makeup and stuff. They looked like Lovely Ladies.

"Nancy," said Kristy, "when is your mom going to have the baby?"

"Any second now," I answered.

"Soon," answered Nancy.

"What are you going to name the baby?" Mary Anne wanted to know.

"She keeps changing her mind," I said.

"Marilyn or Mark," said Nancy.

"Have you ever taken care of a baby?" Claudia asked Nancy.

"No, but I know all about babies."

"Really? Because we could give you some tips on babies and baby-sitting."

"You could?" I cried. "That would be great. I need baby tips. I mean, Nancy does. What do we have to know?"

"Well," said Jessi, "always test the milk

before you give a baby a bottle. Make sure it is not too hot."

"I knew that," said Nancy.

But I did not. I decided to write it down. I might need to know it.

"And never, ever leave a baby alone on the changing table," said Stacey. "He might roll off. Never leave a baby alone in the bath, either."

"I knew that," said Nancy.

I wrote: *Never leave a baby alone.*

"Remember to support the baby's head when you pick him up," said Dawn.

"I knew that," said Nancy.

I wrote: *Support the baby's head.*

"Karen, why are you writing this stuff down?" asked Kristy. She was smiling. "Are you going to baby-sit for Nancy's brother or sister?"

I shrugged. "You never know."

"I do not think you are old enough to baby-sit."

"No, I guess not," I replied. I stuffed the

paper in my pocket. "Come on, let's go," I said to Hannie and Nancy. "We do not want to be pests."

My friends and I left the big kids alone.

Karen's Baby

"Please pass the glue," said Nancy.

I passed her the glue.

"Please pass the glitter," she said.

I passed her the glitter.

"Please pass the . . . the . . ."

"Nancy," I said, "there is nothing left to pass you. Everything is at your end of the table. You are surrounded."

"Oh."

Hannie and Nancy and I giggled. When we had woken up that morning, the morning after the slumber party, we decided to work on our baby presents again. Daddy said Hannie and Nancy could stay until the afternoon.

So my friends and I were busy in the playroom. Nancy was working on her portraits, Hannie was finishing her mobile, and I was starting another bottle-warmer. It was going to look just like the first one, except I would use different colors of felt and yarn.

Suddenly Emily Michelle ran into the room. "I help!" she cried.

"No, Emily!" I did not want Emily to help. She is too messy.

Emily did not pay attention to me. She climbed onto a chair. She took the glue from Nancy. Then she turned the bottle upside down and squeezed.

"Emily! Look what you did! Bad girl!" I scolded her.

And Hannie exclaimed, "She just wrecked part of my mobile!"

"Here," I said. I sat Emily in my lap. I handed her some crayons. "Make a picture. Make your *own* picture," I told her.

"No-no!" Emily jumped up. She grabbed at a pile of felt scraps. She grabbed at a box of markers. She grabbed at a stack of paper.

"Em-i-*lee!*" I shrieked. "Now you are ruining everything. You are messing up all our piles. We just organized our stuff."

"Karen? Does she have to play with us?" asked Nancy.

"No," I replied. I left the table. I ran for Elizabeth. When I told her what Emily was doing, Elizabeth came into the playroom with me.

"Okay, Miss Emily," she said. She lifted her up. "Time to find something else to do. Come downstairs with me."

"No, no, no, no!" cried Emily as Elizabeth carried her to the steps.

"Goodness," said Nancy. "*My* baby will not behave like that."

My friends and I tried to work some more, but we could hear Emily shrieking around the house. "Let's go to your house, Hannie," I said.

So we did.

At Hannie's house we decided to play jacks. Sari sat down with us. Sari is Hannie's little sister. She swatted the jacks and sent them flying.

"No!" cried Hannie.

We decided to watch a video. Sari pressed all the buttons on the VCR.

"No!" cried Hannie.

"*My* baby will not behave like that," said Nancy.

"The new baby will be perfect," I agreed.

"You never know," said Hannie.

That afternoon, Andrew and I returned to the little house. We ate supper with Mommy and Seth. Then I went to my room. I found a piece of paper. I began to make a list. I wrote: Darlene, Maria, Chantal, Rebecca, Hilary, Sue, Christine, Danielle.

Then I made another list. I wrote: Henry, Timothy, Eric, Justin, Brad, Richard, Will. They were lists of names for my baby. Maybe, I thought, if I keep wishing for a baby, and if I plan for a baby, then I will get a baby brother or sister, just like Nancy.

Sisters

I was working on my bottle-warmer again. I had finished the second one. I had started a third at the little house. I could make them pretty fast now. So after school on Monday I was sitting in the playroom at Mommy's. The art materials were spread in front of me. (They were on newspapers, of course. I never forget the newspapers.)

"What are those?" Andrew wanted to know. He was standing next to me. He was peering at my project.

"Bottle-warmers," I told him.

"Oh. Are you going to decorate them?"

"Decorate them?" Hmm. I had not thought of that. I looked at my work. Plain felt sewn together with plain yarn. The bottle-warmers did need decorating. "That is a great idea!" I told Andrew.

"It is? I had a great idea?"

"Yup. Thank you."

I was decorating the bottle-warmers with a glitter pen when Nancy came over.

"Look," I said. "Look at the presents for your baby."

"They are beautiful," replied Nancy. "But what are we going to do with *three* bottle-warmers? We are only going to have one baby."

"Oh, you can always use extras."

I was having fun making those bottle-warmers. I was having fun making hats, too. I had made the first felt hat at Daddy's house. It looked like a beanie. In fact, it looked a little like the hat that went with my Brownie uniform. Only it was not brown. Now I was trying to make other kinds of felt hats. You know something? I had a feeling Nancy's baby would not *really* need so many bottle-warmers and hats. But I had other plans for them.

Nancy sat down across the table from me. She found some Styrofoam balls. She stuck them together with toothpicks. "Look! A snowman!" she said. She glued sequins down his front for buttons.

After awhile, I finished decorating the bottle-warmer. "I better call your mother," I said to Nancy.

Nancy sighed. "The baby is not coming yet."

"It has to come sometime."

I phoned Mrs. Dawes. "Hello," I said. "It's me, Karen."

"Honey, the baby is not here."

"I know, but is he coming?"

"Nope. Not yet."

"Okay. Keep me posted." (Mommy always says that.)

I went back to the playroom.

"No baby," I told Nancy. "Hey, you

know what? Maybe your mother will have twins. Or triplets! Or . . . or . . . What comes after triplets?"

"Quadruplets, I think."

"Yes," I agreed. "Or even quintuplets. Nancy, you could have your very own quints! You could give them names that all start with the same letter. Like Robbie and Rosie and Randy and Regina and Rebecca. And you could dress them in matching outfits."

"Where would they sleep?" asked Nancy.

"In lots of bunk beds. You would be a star at school. Nobody at school has quints in his family."

"Well, maybe quints *would* be fun."

"Of course they would be fun. Gosh, I wonder if anyone has ever given birth to more than five babies. I wonder if you could have seven or eight. Wouldn't that be cool? Nancy? Wouldn't you like to have eight little sisters?"

"I do not think so," said Nancy.

Bears and Balloons

The next day, Mrs. Dawes picked up Nancy and me at school. Nancy and I usually carpool, since we live next door to each other.

I was a little surprised to see Mrs. Dawes. I was expecting Mommy or Seth to pick us up. I was pretty sure Mrs. Dawes had gone to the hospital to have the baby. But the baby was not coming yet. Goodness, this baby was a slowpoke.

"Girls," said Mrs. Dawes as she was driving us home, "guess what I am going to do this afternoon."

"Have the baby?" I asked. "Is the baby coming?"

Mrs. Dawes did not really even answer me. She said, "I am going to pick out things for the baby's room."

"Cool!" said Nancy. "You mean the furniture?"

"I mean everything. Everything the baby will need. Furniture, diapers, clothes, toys. We have to get ready for when he comes." Mrs. Dawes glanced at me in the mirror.

I was very good. I did not ask *when* the baby was going to come.

"Who would like to go to the store with me?" asked Mrs. Dawes.

"Me! Me!" Nancy and I cried. And Nancy added, "Can we invite Hannie, too? This is important, Mommy. The Three Musketeers should be together. Hannie would not want to miss this."

"Okay," agreed Mrs. Dawes. "An adventure for the Three Musketeers."

Later that afternoon Mrs. Dawes drove Nancy and me to Hannie's house. We picked up Hannie. Then we drove to the baby store downtown. That store is wonderful. It has only things for babies. And it has any baby thing you could think of.

When Hannie and Nancy and I stepped inside we stopped and stared.

"Oh," Hannie whispered.

"This is like a baby museum," I whispered.

"Why are you whispering?" asked Nancy.

We shrugged.

Mrs. Dawes said, "Before we start shopping, why don't you girls decide on a theme for the room. Maybe animals. Or the seashore. Think of something a boy *or* a girl would like."

After a long discussion, my friends and I decided on teddy bears and balloons.

And then the fun began.

"Furniture first," said Mrs. Dawes.

We picked out a crib, a dresser, a changing table, and a rocking chair. Each one was decorated with a picture of a teddy bear. Then we found a lamp with a bear on it. The bear was holding a bunch of balloons.

"Now for baby supplies," said Nancy's mother.

We picked out crib sheets, blankets, a car seat, a stroller, a highchair, an infant seat, and a walker for when the baby is older.

"Clothes," said Nancy's mother.

Undershirts, socks, sleepers, a snowsuit, a hat, plus diapers and bibs.

"Toys," said Nancy's mother.

Teddy bear, mobile, two rattles, and a music box.

"Yikes," I said. "I did not know babies needed so much."

Nancy's mother was talking to the salesman who had helped us. "You can deliver everything?" I heard her say.

"When? When will it be delivered?" I

cried. "I want to set up the baby's room right away."

"Oh, we can't do that, honey," said Mrs. Dawes. "The things will be delivered *after* the baby is born. Then we will set up the room."

"Boo," I said. But now I had a new project. I was going to make a list of things *my* baby would need.

Going to the Hospital

"**M**ush, mush, mush. I am making mushed potatoes," said Andrew.

"Andrew, please stop playing with your food," said Mommy.

It was dinnertime at the little house, and Andrew was being a slob. A week had gone by since my friends and I had picked out the baby things. But the baby was still not on the way.

Ring, ring!

"Darn it!" said Mommy. "Why do people always call while we are eating?"

"I'll get it," said Seth.

Seth ran into the kitchen. When he came back to the table he was smiling. "We better set another place," he said. "Guess who was on the phone."

"Who?" I asked.

"Mr. Dawes. The baby is coming. He is about to drive Nancy's mother to the hospital. Nancy is going to spend the night here. She's on her way over."

"She is? She is?" I leaped out of my chair. I almost knocked it over. "The baby is coming!" I cried. I danced around the table. "The baby is coming! The baby is coming! The baby is coming! And Nancy and I are going to have a sleepover on a school night! I never had a sleepover on a school night!"

"Karen." Mommy caught me by the arm as I whizzed by her. "My goodness. Please settle down. And use your indoor voice. If you cannot calm down, you and Nancy will have to sleep in separate rooms tonight."

Uh-oh. I stood quietly by Mommy's chair. "I promise I will be good," I whispered.

"Thank you," she whispered back.

A few minutes later, Nancy rang our doorbell. She was carrying her bookbag and an overnight bag and her best doll.

"Look," she said. "There go Mommy and Daddy."

I saw the Daweses' car backing down their driveway.

"I wonder how long it takes for a baby to be born," I said.

"I don't know. Daddy told me he would call tonight."

"We will know before we go to sleep!" I exclaimed.

After dinner, Mommy helped Nancy get settled in my room. Then Nancy and I decided to work on our baby presents. I had quite a few. I had made a tall pile of bottle-warmers, and a shorter pile of felt hats. Nancy had made three mobiles and three pairs of felt booties.

"What are we going to do with all this stuff?" asked Nancy.

"Well — " I began, but the phone rang.

"Daddy!" shrieked Nancy. But the caller was Kristy.

Nancy and I went back to the baby things.

"I have never seen so much baby stuff. Except in that store," said Nancy.

Ring, ring!

"Daddy!"

This time the caller was some friend of Seth's.

The third time the phone rang, it was for Andrew. He never gets phone calls.

"Who was that?" I asked him.

"My friend Alicia. She invited me to her birthday party."

Lucky duck.

The fourth time the phone rang, it was . . . Mr. Dawes.

"Aughh!" Nancy shrieked.

"You are a big sister now!" I shrieked.

Guess what Mr. Dawes said to Nancy.

He said, "Honey, the baby is on his way, but he is not here yet. And it is getting late. It is time for you to go to bed. So I will call you before you leave for school tomorrow morning. I promise."

"Okay," said Nancy. "Good night."

And I said, "Nancy, your baby is a Giant Slowpoke."

Daniel

I did not sleep very much that night. Mr. Dawes had said he would call in the morning. But I thought he might change his mind. Maybe the baby would be born and Mr. Dawes would be so excited he would call anyway. Long after Mommy turned out my light, I lay in bed thinking.

"Nancy? Nancy?" I said after awhile. But Nancy did not answer. She was asleep. How could she sleep at a time like this?

I turned over in bed. I closed my eyes. I began to count babies. After about one hundred babies I fell asleep.

On Wednesday, Nancy and I woke up before Mommy came into my room.

"Today you become a big sister!" I announced. "How do you feel?"

"Important," said Nancy proudly.

The phone rang during breakfast. We all looked at each other.

"That *must* be your father, honey," Mommy said to Nancy. "You answer it."

Nancy grabbed for the phone. "Hello?" she cried. "Hi, Daddy . . . I am? . . . I do? . . . You will? . . . I can? . . . Oh, thank you! I will tell you the name I chose when I see you. I want to surprise you. Tell Mommy I love her. . . . What? . . . Oh, okay." Nancy held the phone away from her ear. "Daddy wants to talk to you," she said to Mommy.

Then she sat down.

"Nancy, what is it? Do you have a

brother or a sister? I am going to explode!"
I said.

Nancy grinned. "It's a boy!" she exclaimed. "I'm a big sister! I'm a big sister, and I have a baby brother. I decided to name him Daniel. I changed my mind one last time," she added. "Guess what. Daddy is going to pick me up after school and take me to the hospital. I will get to meet Daniel. Oh, and the store is going to deliver the baby stuff today. I think that is what my daddy and your mommy are talking about."

Seth drove Nancy and me to school that morning. We ran inside and all the way to Ms. Colman's room, even though we are not supposed to run in the halls. We could not help ourselves.

Nancy told her news to all the kids in our room. "I am a big sister," she announced. "My mommy had the baby last night. It is a boy. I named him Daniel. I get to visit him this afternoon. I am going to hold him and feed him and change him. I know I will be the best big sister ever. Soon I will bring Daniel in for Show and Share. Then you can see him in person."

Oh, I cannot wait until I am a big sister myself.

The Littlest Baby

When school ended, Nancy and I ran outside. We looked at the line of cars waiting to drive kids home. We saw Nancy's daddy and my mommy. We both ran to Mr. Dawes's car. I just had to talk to him.

"Hi, Karen," said Mr. Dawes.

"Hi! How is Mrs. Dawes? How is the baby?"

"They are both fine. They will be home soon. Maybe even tomorrow."

"Tomorrow! Yea!" That was sooner than I had thought.

When I was sitting in our car with Mommy, I said, "How come Nancy gets to see Daniel? I thought children were not allowed to visit people in the hospital. I thought we were too young."

"Sometimes children are allowed to visit," replied Mommy. "In special cases. And babies are special cases. It is important for brothers and sisters to get to know each other as soon as possible. So there is a new rule at the hospital. Older brothers and sisters can visit the new babies and their moms late in the afternoon. A special visiting time for kids."

"Oh. . . . Mommy, what am I going to do at home today while I wait for Nancy to come back? I cannot think about anything except Daniel."

"You can watch for the delivery truck," said Mommy. "It has not come yet. Then you and I can go next door and tell the driver to leave the boxes and packages in Nancy's garage. We can watch the driver unload the truck."

When we got home I sat outside on our front steps. But not for long. The air was too cold. I even saw some snowflakes. So Andrew and I watched from the living room. We waited and waited.

"Here is the truck!" I yelled finally.

Mommy and Andrew and I ran next door. We watched a man and a woman take box after box after box out of the truck. They piled them into the garage. They did not leave any room for Mr. Dawes's car.

Just before dinnertime, Nancy's father brought Nancy back to the little house. "I will see you later," he said to her. "I will come back after dinner, in time for you to go to sleep in your own bed."

"Okay," said Nancy. " 'Bye, Daddy."

"Nancy, Nancy! Tell me everything about Daniel!" I begged.

"Maybe later," said Nancy.

"I think Nancy is tired," said Mommy. "Ask her about Daniel at dinner."

At dinner I said, "Okay, Nancy. Now tell

us about Daniel. What is he like?"

Nancy shrugged.

"Do your parents like his name?"

"I guess."

Nancy would not tell us about her baby brother.

Later, Nancy and I went upstairs to my room. "What is wrong?" I asked. "Why won't you talk about Daniel?"

Nancy began to cry. "Because I am afraid of him, that's why. He is the littlest baby I have ever seen. He looks like he might break. I'm afraid I will drop him or hurt him. And guess what. He probably *is* coming home tomorrow afternoon. I do not want him home so soon, Karen."

I did not know what to say to Nancy. I did not understand her. I wanted a baby and I could not have one. Nancy had a baby and she did not want him. Boo.

After awhile I said, "Hey, Nancy! I have an idea! This will cheer you up. I know what to do with all our baby stuff. We can sell it! We almost have enough for a store of our own. What do you think?"

Nancy shrugged. "I cannot think about anything except Daniel. Anyway, I have to pack my things. Daddy will be here soon."

Daniel's Mezuzah

When Mommy picked up Nancy and me after school the next day, she had some news. It was good news for Nancy and bad news for me. "Nancy," said Mommy, "your father called me today. Your mother and Daniel are going to come home tomorrow, not this afternoon."

"Yea!" cried Nancy.

"Boo," I said.

Then Nancy asked, "Why?"

"Your mother is tired," said Mommy. "She just needs a little extra rest. Oh, your father wants to know if you want to visit Daniel this afternoon."

"No, thank you," Nancy answered politely.

"Mommy, what are we going to *do* this afternoon?" I whined. "I thought Nancy and I would be able to play with the baby."

"Guess what. Mr. Dawes has a job for you two. He hoped you would want to put away the baby's things. He unpacked the furniture this morning, but nothing else. And now he is at the hospital again."

"Nancy, we can set up Daniel's room!" I cried. "That would be fun. Wouldn't it? Please, Nancy?"

Nancy smiled a little. "Okay. I guess it would be fun," she said.

Kristy came to Nancy's house that afternoon. She stayed with Nancy and me, and helped us unpack the boxes.

"Oh, look! Here is Daniel's lamp!" I cried. Kristy and I lifted the teddy bear lamp out of its box.

"It's so cute!" exclaimed Kristy.

"Here are Daniel's toys," I said later.

Nancy peered at them. "See, Kristy?" she said. "The music box plays 'The Teddy Bears' Picnic.' And here is a mobile. We can hang it over the crib. I think Hannie made another mobile for Daniel. We can hang that one over the changing table. Oh, here. Let's put the teddy bear in the rocking chair."

Nancy took charge. "Next let's fill up the dresser," she said.

We put away Daniel's clothes.

"Now let's set up the changing table."

We unpacked Baby Wipes and diapers and lotion and powder.

Just when I thought Daniel's room looked perfect, Nancy said, "I almost forgot. One more thing. Mommy and I picked this out. Daddy bought it yesterday." Nancy ran to her room. When she came back she was holding something small. It was packed in tissue paper. Nancy unwrapped the paper. Inside was an ornament. It looked like Noah's Ark.

"What's that?" asked Kristy.

"It is Daniel's mezuzah," said Nancy. "Daddy is going to put it right here." She pointed to a spot on the door frame. "Mezuzah means doorpost," she said. "In Hebrew. See that little piece of paper inside the ark? All rolled up? It has some Bible passages written on it. And *Shaddai*. That means the Almighty."

"Nancy has one by her door, too," I told Kristy. "And there is one on the front door of the house. The papers inside are the same, but the cases are different. Right, Nancy?" I said proudly.

"Right," she agreed.

Nancy showed Kristy her mezuzah. Then the three of us looked at Daniel's room again. We thought it was perfect. But just to be sure, Nancy and I tested it with our baby dolls. They seemed to like everything.

Now all Daniel's room needed was Daniel.

Hats for Sale

The next day was Friday. Daniel was going to come home that afternoon. On Friday morning, Nancy and Hannie and I went to school carrying big paper bags. The bags were full. They were full of baby things. Bottle-warmers and hats and booties and mobiles.

We planned to sell them in school.

A couple of years ago, Hannie and Nancy and I had a favorite picture book. It was called *Caps for Sale*. We loved the story about the man who sold caps and wore all the caps on his head in one tall, tall tower. He would walk through town calling, "Caps! Caps for sale! Fifty cents a cap!"

So before school that morning, the Three Musketeers walked up and down the rows of desks in Ms. Colman's room. We held out our piles of baby things. I called, "Hats! Hats for sale! Fifty cents a hat!" And, "Bottle-warmers for sale! Fifty cents a bottle-warmer!"

Nancy called, "Booties for sale! Fifty cents apiece! A dollar for a pair!"

And Hannie called, "Mobiles for sale! A buck will get you one!"

Bobby Gianelli looked at our stuff. "A buck for a mobile?" he repeated. "That is a lot of money. I would not spend a dollar on one of your old mobiles."

"It takes a long time to make a mobile," said Hannie.

"It takes a long time to earn a dollar," replied Bobby.

Then Ricky Torres looked at our things. "Who needs bottle-warmers, anyway?" he said. He went back to his game of marbles.

Now Bobby is a big bully. I would expect him to say something rude. But Ricky is my pretend husband. We got married on the playground one afternoon. *He* was not supposed to be rude to us.

I walked over to a bunch of girls. "Hats for sale!" I cried.

Pamela Harding looked at the baby beanies. She made a face. "Who made those?" she said. "Your little brother?"

No wonder Pamela is my best enemy.

Nobody wanted to buy our baby things. By the time Ms. Colman came in the room, the Three Musketeers had not earned a single penny.

I think maybe Ms. Colman felt sorry for us. At lunchtime she said, "Girls, why don't you bring your things to the teachers' room. You might have some customers there. Come with me."

We did have some customers!

Mrs. Klein looked at the booties. "Adorable," she said. She bought a pair.

Mr. Peterson looked at the mobiles. "My daughter would love these," he said. He bought a pink and white mobile.

And Ms. Colman looked at the hats. "Lovely," she said. "I will take one."

"Pamela thought my little brother made them," I told her.

"Well, I think they are very nice," she replied.

The Three Musketeers had sold one pair of booties, one mobile, and one hat. We had earned two dollars and fifty cents.

"I bet a store earns more than that in one day," I said.

"They probably don't have so many things left over at the end of the day, either," said Hannie.

"I wonder what we are doing wrong," said Nancy.

"Maybe we don't have enough to choose from. Maybe we need to sell more *kinds* of baby things," I suggested.

"Maybe," said Hannie and Nancy.

At least the day had passed quickly. I had thought it would be lo-o-o-o-ong and slo-o-o-o-ow. But it was not too bad.

When the bell did ring, I cried, "Here we come, Daniel!"

The Sad News

The Three Musketeers ran out of school together. We saw my mommy in her car and Hannie's mommy in her car. We all ran to my mommy first.

"Is Daniel home?" asked Hannie. "Is he home yet?"

"Not yet," said Mommy.

"Boo," said the Three Musketeers.

Then Hannie said, "I have to go. Someone call me when Daniel comes home, okay? I want to know the minute he is home."

"Okay," Nancy and I promised.

That afternoon, Nancy and I sat in the living room at the little house. We sat by the window. We held our dolls in our laps.

We waited and waited and waited. We did not see the Daweses' car.

After a long time, the phone rang. Mommy answered it. When she hung up, she called, "Nancy? Karen? Can you come here, please?"

We ran into the kitchen.

"Girls," said Mommy, "I have some sad news. Daniel is not feeling very well, so he will not be coming home this afternoon."

Nancy looked scared. "What's the matter with him?" she asked.

"Nothing too serious," said Mommy. "A couple of little problems. One of them is called jaundice. Lots of babies get that. They just need to stay in the hospital for a few extra days. When Daniel does come home, he will be feeling fine."

"Okay," said Nancy. She looked as scared as ever. "Is Mommy coming home?"

"Tomorrow. She could come home today, but your daddy said she wanted to spend one more night at the hospital with Daniel. Also, your daddy is going to be at the hospital until late tonight, Nancy, so you are going to stay with Karen again."

"But it is Friday!" I exclaimed. "I am going to the big house."

"And Nancy will go with you. I'm sure it will be fine with your father and Elizabeth. I am going to call them right now. But I already told Mr. Dawes that's where Nancy would be. Is that okay with you, Nancy?"

Nancy nodded.

"Yes!" I cried. "We can have another sleepover tonight! Only it will be better than the last one because we will not have to wake up early."

Nancy nodded again.

Then Mommy took us next door so Nancy could pack some things for our slumber party. We passed by Daniel's room. We all looked inside. But nobody said anything. Until later. On our way to the big house, Mommy said, "I know you are sad, girls. But you do not need to worry. I am sure Daniel will be fine."

I took Mommy's advice. I did not worry.

Nancy worried, though. At dinner, she hardly said a word.

Nannie said, "Nancy, you are a big sister now. How does that feel?"

"Fine."

And Kristy said, "I love the name Daniel. Is that your favorite name?"

"I guess."

And Daddy said, "What did you think when you saw your brother?"

"He's okay."

After that, everyone stopped asking Nancy questions.

Nancy was no fun at our slumber party. She did not want to play games with me. She did not want to play Lovely Ladies. She did not want to raid the refrigerator. All she wanted to do was read.

"Are you okay, Nancy?" I asked.

"No. I am not okay. I *told* you Daniel was little and scary. Now he is sick. How are we going to take care of him? It will be too hard. He is *so* tiny. Maybe he will never come home from the hospital."

The Baby Sale

Nancy felt better the next morning. Her father called her. He said, "Nancy, I am going to the hospital again now, but Mommy and I will both come home after lunch. We will pick you up at Karen's then."

"How is Daniel?" asked Nancy.

"He's doing fine. The doctor said he can probably go home on Tuesday. That is just three days from now. How would you like to go out to dinner tonight? You and mommy and me?"

"Tonight? Don't you have to be with Daniel?"

"We want to be with you."

"All *right!*" cried Nancy. When she hung up the phone, she said, "What shall we do this morning, Karen? We can play all morning."

"Hmm," I said. "Maybe we should try having another baby sale. This time we can sell our baby things to the neighbors. We can walk from door to door and say, 'Would you like to buy one of our lovely items?' "

"Okay," replied Nancy. "Except I left all my lovely items at home."

"That's all right. Some of my things are here at the big house. And Hannie has her things."

I telephoned Hannie. She came right over with six mobiles and a drawing of Noah's Ark. "Isn't my picture beautiful?" she said. "It will be a perfect decoration for a baby's room."

The Three Musketeers piled their things in my red wagon. Then we put on our coats. We were ready for our baby sale.

"Where are you going?" called Elizabeth.

When I told her, she said, "Ask Kristy or a grown-up to go with you."

Kristy came with us. She walked behind the wagon and made sure nothing fell out. Hannie and Nancy and I took turns pulling the wagon.

We went across the street to Hannie's house first.

Hannie rang her bell. When her mother came to the door, I said, "Hello. We are having a baby sale. Would you like to buy a lovely item?"

"We-ell," said Mrs. Papadakis.

"How about a lovely mobile?" asked Hannie.

Mrs. Papadakis sighed. Then she bought one mobile.

While we were walking next door to the Kilbournes' house, Kristy said, "Are you guys sure you want to call this a baby sale? It sounds as if you are selling babies." She frowned.

"Well, we are selling baby *things*," I told her. Even so, when Mr. Kilbourne answered the door, I said, "Hello, we are having a baby-things sale. Would you like to buy a lovely item?"

"You are having a what?" replied Mr. Kilbourne.

"A baby-things sale."

Mr. Kilbourne did not buy any baby things.

"I should have said we were having a baby sale," I whined as we left the house. "Just like I had planned."

"Sorry," said Kristy.

Next we rang Melody Korman's doorbell. Melody is a friend of ours, even though she does not go to our school.

Melody was not at home, but her mother was. Mrs. Korman answered the door holding Melody's baby sister. When we told her about the baby sale, she smiled. Then she bought the picture of Noah's Ark.

"This is just what Skylar's room needs," she said.

At twelve o'clock we stopped our sale. Kristy pulled the wagon home because the Three Musketeers were very tired. Also, we had only earned two more dollars.

But Nancy was grinning. She could not wait to see her mother.

Waiting for Daniel

Here is some gigundoly good news. On Monday Nancy said to me, "Karen, guess what. Daniel is going to come home tomorrow."

"Yes!" I cried. "Does that mean he is all well?"

"It means he is very well, and that tomorrow he will be all well."

Nancy's mother had come home on Saturday. I saw her on Sunday evening when Andrew and I returned to the little house.

I was surprised because Mrs. Dawes was still fat. Not *quite* as fat as before she had Daniel, but still fat. Plus, she looked tired.

I asked Mommy about this and she said Mrs. Dawes would look the same as usual before I knew it. She said to be patient.

There are just so many things to be patient about.

The hardest one was the baby, of course. Waiting for Daniel.

"Are you still scared?" I asked Nancy in school on Monday.

"A little. Not as much. Mommy and Daddy told me to remember something. They said to remember that I am Daniel's big sister, but that I only have to *help* take care of him. They will do the hard things. If anything scares me, Mommy or Daddy will handle it. Then we will talk about it."

"What time is Daniel coming home?" I asked.

"In the morning," said Nancy. "Early."

"Before we leave for school?" Hannie wanted to know.

"Not that early. But he will be waiting for me after school."

"We should do something special for Daniel," I said. "When we adopted Emily Michelle, we made a big sign that said *Welcome, Emily*. And we baked cookies for her. It was a very special day."

"Let's make a sign for Daniel," said Nancy. "Can you guys come to my house after school? Mommy said she would be at home."

The Three Musketeers worked very hard on the sign. It said WELCOME HOME, DANIEL! We drew each letter on a separate piece of paper. We even used one whole piece of paper for the !. Then we strung the papers together. Mrs. Dawes helped us hang them over the fireplace.

"There. All ready for Daniel," said Hannie.

"Now if he would just come home," I added.

"He will be here before you know it," said Mrs. Dawes.

"At last I will feel like a big sister," said Nancy.

Welcome Home, Daniel!

"Today is the big day!" I cried. The Three Musketeers had just reached school. When we saw each other, we jumped up and down. Then we ran to Ms. Colman's room.

"How will we wait? How will we wait all day?" I asked.

I tried to be a good waiter. I really did. But I was a little bit wiggly. Also, Ms. Colman had to tell me twice to remember to use my indoor voice. And both times she had to interrupt the class to do it.

I felt sorry. But I just could not keep still.

"Maybe we should not be too excited," said Hannie at lunchtime. "What if he does not come home after all? What if Daniel has to stay at the hospital for another day or two?"

"He will come home today," said Nancy. "I just know it."

The Three Musketeers rode home from school together. Mommy picked us up.

"Is Daniel home?" asked Nancy.

Guess what. He was not.

"But he will be later this afternoon. Your parents are at the hospital now, Nancy. I'm not sure what the delay was," said Mommy. "Why don't you girls play outside and watch for the car. You can take Andrew with you."

We did not *really* want to play with Andrew, but we played with him anyway. After our snack we put on jackets and mittens and scarves and hats and boots. We ran into the front yard. We tried to build a snowman but there was not enough snow. So we made a snowman head. Then we sat on our steps and counted cars. Andrew saw the Daweses' car first.

"There it is!" he shrieked.

"This is it! Here's Daniel!" I cried.

"He's home!" added Nancy.

Hannie and Nancy and Andrew and I ran next door. We watched the car pull into the driveway. We watched Mr. Dawes park it carefully. We watched him help Mrs. Dawes out. She was holding a bundle of blankets. That is all I could see. Just some soft blankets.

"Where is he?" I whispered.

My friends and I had crowded around Mrs. Dawes.

"He's right here," she answered.

Nancy stood on tiptoe. She peered into the blankets. "Hi, Daniel," she said softly. "It's me, Nancy. Your big sister."

Then Hannie and Andrew and I peered into the blankets. And there was a teeny, tiny face. A doll's face. Soft and pink. Daniel was asleep.

"Let's go inside now, kids," said Mr.

Dawes. "It's cold out here."

When we were inside, we took off our coats. We sat in the living room. Nancy and her mother sat on the couch. Mrs. Dawes let Nancy hold Daniel. Now that he was not so wrapped up, I could see him better. And Nancy had been right. He was very, very small. I do not remember Andrew when he was that small. Daniel was not much bigger than Hyacynthia, my best doll baby.

Mr. Dawes brought two cameras into the living room, a video camera and a regular one. He took some pictures of Andrew and the Three Musketeers looking at Daniel. Then he took about a thousand pictures of Mrs. Dawes and Nancy holding Daniel.

"Let's show Daniel his room," said Nancy after awhile.

Mrs. Dawes picked up Daniel. We followed her to Daniel's bedroom. Mr. Dawes followed us with the video camera.

"Here you go, Daniel," said Nancy. "This is your room. Welcome home."

Kristy

After I saw Daniel, I decided something. I decided I just had to have a baby of my own. A baby brother or sister. I did not care which.

One evening, Kristy came to baby-sit at the little house. Mommy and Seth were going to a party. "Have fun with Kristy," said Mommy as she put on her coat. "Do what she tells you. Andrew, your bedtime is eight-thirty. Karen, yours is nine, but you may read in bed for half an hour. Lights out at nine-thirty."

"Okay," said Andrew and I.

We could not wait for Mommy and Seth to leave. As soon as they did, Andrew said, "Let's play Candy Land!"

I said, "Let's put on a play."

We did both things. Then Kristy made cocoa. And then Andrew had to go to bed. While Kristy read a story to Andrew, I looked over my baby lists. I had started quite a few. There were my lists of names, of course. They were getting pretty long. Then there was a list of baby furniture, a list of baby toys, a list of baby clothes, a list of picture books, and a list of ways to decorate my baby's room. (My favorite was Animals Around the World.)

I did not hear Kristy come into my room.

"Karen?" she said.

I jumped. "You scared me!"

"Sorry. I just put Andrew to bed. What are all those?"

"These? These lists?" I tried to hide them, but Kristy had already seen them.

"Furniture For My Baby," she read. "Books For My Baby. What baby, Karen? You mean your imaginary baby, don't you? Because you know you are not going to get a *real* baby brother or sister."

"Well, I *sort* of meant a real one," I admitted.

"But, Karen, everyone has told you and told you. You are probably not going to get a new brother or sister. Your mom and Seth do not plan to have a baby, and neither do your dad and my mom. . . . Karen, do you want to have a baby, or do you want to be a big sister?"

"Both, I guess."

Well, Daniel is right next door. You can visit him a lot. And you already *are* a big sister. You have a little sister *and* a little brother."

"I know. But they are not babies."

"No, but they are fun. They can *do* things. You can color with Emily, and you taught Andrew to read. Remember that?

You could not teach a baby to read."

"Babies wear diapers," I said. "They need to be taken care of."

"Emily still wears diapers most of the time," Kristy pointed out. "You are welcome to change her stinky diapers whenever you want."

I giggled. "Okay, but it is not the same."

"I know," Kristy replied. "Hey, how is your baby sale going?"

"We still have most of the stuff."

"Too bad. Can I look at it again?"

"Sure!" I said. "I only have my things, though. The bottle-warmers and the hats. And I tried to make two mobiles, but mine are not as good as Hannie's or Nancy's."

I spread the things on my bed.

Kristy looked at them for a long time. At last she said, "You know, I could use some of these things when I baby-sit. I should bring them in the Kid-Kit I carry. They would come in handy." Kristy bought two bottle-warmers, one hat, and one mobile. "My friends might want to buy some things, too," she said. "They all take care of babies sometimes. You know, Karen, you should sell your things to people who either work with babies or have babies of their own."

Oh! What an idea! Of course. Hannie and Nancy and I had mostly been selling to the wrong people, but I would take care of that. It was time to go back into business with the right people.

Danny

Nancy's brother had been home for one whole week. I had not held him yet, but Mrs. Dawes said I could soon. She did not let very many people hold him. She said she had to be careful of germs.

When Daniel had been home for two weeks, Nancy said to me, "I do not think he looks as awfully tiny as he used to, do you?"

I shook my head. No. But Daniel was still very little.

"I have given him a few bottles," said

Nancy proudly. She was not afraid of her brother anymore. "I feel like he has always been here," she added. "Daniel is part of the family. Guess what. He has a nickname now."

"He does?

"Yes. We call him Danny."

"Danny," I repeated. "That's nice. I like that."

One day, when Danny had been home for quite a few weeks, Nancy called me on the phone. "Guess what, guess what, guess what!" she cried.

"What? Tell me!"

"Mommy said I can bring Danny to school for Show and Share!"

"Really?" I could not believe it. Nancy would have the best Show and Share ever. Nobody had brought in a real, live baby before.

Ms. Colman set up a special Show and Share, just for Danny. She asked Mrs. Dawes what would be a good time to bring the baby in. I guess she did not want to interrupt one of Danny's naps.

Mrs. Dawes brought Danny to school on a Friday morning. Before she arrived, Ms. Colman talked to our class. "Remember that Danny is very little," she said.

"Not as little as he used to be!" interrupted Nancy. Nancy was a teensy bit too excited about Show and Share.

"But still small," Ms. Colman went on. "So please keep your voices down. And stay in your seats. If you crowd around Danny you may frighten him. Don't worry. You will all get a chance to see him."

When Mrs. Dawes knocked on the door to our room, we were very, very quiet. Nancy opened the door. She let her mother inside. "Welcome to school, Mommy," she said. "Welcome to school, Danny. Thank you for coming. I hope your stay will be pleasant." (Nancy had been rehearsing this speech.) "Please take a seat in our special visitor's chair."

The special visitor's chair was really just Ms. Colman's chair. Nancy had moved it to the front of the room. Her own chair was next to it. She and her mother sat down, side by side. Mrs. Dawes held Danny.

Danny looked quite handsome. Nancy had picked out his outfit that morning. She had chosen red overalls, a striped shirt, and white socks. (Danny usually does not wear shoes.)

"This," said Nancy, "is my mother." (Mrs. Dawes smiled.) "And this is Danny, my new baby brother. Who has a question about Danny?"

Natalie Springer raised her hand. "Do you get to hold him?" she asked.

"Sure," answered Nancy. "I hold him a lot."

I raised my hand. "I have held him four times," I told the class.

"What do you do when he cries?" asked Ricky Torres.

"I have to find out what he wants," said Nancy.

"Like maybe he needs a fresh diaper," I added.

"I have a question for *Nancy*," said Pamela. "Can Danny laugh yet?"

"Yes. He laughs when you tickle him," said Nancy. "And you know what? Karen can always make him laugh. Karen is like another sister for Danny."

I grinned. I liked that idea.

Later, Mrs. Dawes walked around the room so everyone could look at Danny. When she stopped at my desk, I tickled Danny and made him laugh.

The Dirty Diaper

I twirled the mobile over Danny's crib. "Look! Look at those shapes, Danny," I said. "Watch them move."

Fuss, fuss, fuss. Danny did not smile. He crumpled up his face.

"Is he crying again, Karen?" called Nancy.

"He is about to. Hurry up with his clothes. Maybe he is cold."

Nancy and I were baby-sitting for Danny. We were in his bedroom. Mrs. Dawes was in the living room. She had just changed

Danny. Now we were letting her take a break. We baby-sat for Danny like that as often as we could.

Nancy ran to the crib. "Here is his sleeper," she said.

As soon as Nancy began to put the sleeper on her brother, he started to fuss again. I twirled the mobile some more. Then I said, "Here is a new song, Danny. I do not think you have heard it before." I sang, "I'm a little teapot, short and stout. Here is my handle, here is my spout."

Danny kicked his legs. He frowned.

"Don't you like the song?" I asked.

And Nancy said, "Hold still, Danny."

I wished Danny could sing along with me, but of course he could not. He could not even talk. Once, I thought I heard him say da-da, but it might have been a mistake. Mr. Dawes was nowhere nearby.

"What is the matter with your brother today?" I asked.

Nancy sighed. "I don't know. He is fussy. Sometimes he just gets fussy."

"You know what?" I said. "We have not played Lovely Ladies in ages, Nancy. We have not played with our dolls, either."

"That is because we have a real baby," Nancy replied.

When Danny was finally ready, Nancy called, "Mommy! He's dressed!"

I sniffed the air. "Hey, Nancy," I said. "I smell something."

"Yuck," said Nancy. "Me, too." We looked at each other. We made faces. "Dirty diaper!" we shrieked.

"What?" said Mrs. Dawes.

"Mommy, you just changed him and already he has a dirty diaper," complained Nancy. "He is a mess."

He was even messier after Mrs. Dawes fed him later. She held him up to her shoulder, burped him, and —

"Ew! Ew, gross!" I cried. "He spit up!"

It was one of Danny's disgusting days. He has them every now and then.

Nancy and I changed his outfit *again* and he fussed some more.

Boy. Andrew and Emily are much more fun than Danny, I thought. And they are not nearly as messy. Oh, well. I could look forward to when Danny was older. He would be neater *and* I could teach him songs. But that would not be for awhile. Not for months. Maybe even a couple of years.

I decided I was glad Danny lived next door, and not in my house. Maybe I did not need a real baby of my own after all.

"Nancy," I said, "I think I am going to go home now." I wanted to leave before Danny spit up again.

Back at the little house, I went into my bedroom. I closed the door. I opened my desk drawer. Inside were my baby lists. I spread them out and looked at them. And then I threw them away, except for the lists of baby names. I liked those lists. But I knew I did not need the others.

After that I decided it was time for a new project. The Three Musketeers had not made any baby things in ages. Guess what.

We had sold all the things we had made. Kristy's friends had bought a lot of them. The rest were bought by people who actually had babies.

Maybe I would go into the jewelry business. That would be a good new project.

The Fairy Godsister

One Saturday, I was in the rec room at the little house. I was busy making jewelry. I was stringing tiny beads onto elastic strings for s-t-r-e-t-c-h-y bracelets and necklaces. Andrew was coloring in a coloring book. He was not staying in the lines.

When the phone rang, I yelled, "I'll get it!"

"Indoor voice, Karen," Mommy reminded me.

"Sorry," I whispered. I picked up the phone. "Hello?"

"Hi, Karen. It is me," said Nancy. "Can you come over right away?"

"Right away?" I repeated. "Is something wrong?"

Nancy giggled. "Nope. *Can* you come over?" She sounded excited.

"Sure. I will be — "

"Wear a dress," Nancy interrupted me. "I cannot tell you why. Just wear one. And please hurry. 'Bye!" She hung up.

This was very mysterious.

I ran upstairs to my room. I changed into my best party dress and my black clickety-clack Mary Jane shoes. I tied a ribbon in my hair. Then I told Mommy where I was going. I raced to Nancy's house. I rang the doorbell.

Nancy opened the door right away. She must have been waiting for me. "Hi!" she said. She was as dressed up as I was. And she was holding Danny, who was wearing his very best outfit.

"What is going on?" I asked.

"I have a surprise for you," said Nancy. "Come on in."

Nancy led me into the living room. She pointed to an armchair. "You sit there," she said. "That is the seat for the guest of honor."

I sat down. Nancy handed me Danny. She placed him in my arms.

"Why are we all dressed up?" I asked.

"You will find out." Nancy ran out of the living room. When she came back she was carrying a crown. I could tell she had made it herself. She had cut it out of yellow paper. She had glued sparkles on each point. And she had written KAREN with a glitter pen.

"It is not my birthday," I said. "It is not a holiday."

"Yes, it is," replied Nancy. "It is sort of a holiday. Oh, wait a second. I forgot my magic wand." Nancy left the room again.

I looked down at Danny. "What is your sister doing?" I asked him.

Danny smiled and kicked his feet. Then he drooled on my arm.

"Yuck," I said as Nancy came back.

Nancy stood in front of me. She set the crown on my head. Then she waved the magic wand around. (The wand was a stick with a star glued to one end.) "Karen," said Nancy, and she sounded very solemn, "I know you wanted a baby brother or sister of your own. And I got one and you did not. You really have been like another big sister to Danny. You play with him, but you help with the yucky things, too."

"That is true," I agreed. "Just now, he drooled on me."

Nancy nodded. (She handed me a Kleenex.) Then she said, "Karen, do you promise to love Danny like he is your very own baby brother?"

"Yes," I replied.

"Do you promise to help me teach him to ride a bike?"

"Yes."

"Do you promise to help me protect him from bullies?"

"Yes."

"Then I now pronounce you Danny's fairy godsister."

"His fairy godsister?" I repeated. "You mean like the fairy godmother in *Cinderella*?"

"Yes," replied Nancy, "except that you are real."

Ooh. This was so exciting. I was wearing a crown and holding a baby and one of my best friends had just made me a fairy godsister. I was so happy that I wanted to leap around and use my outdoor voice. Instead, I looked down at Danny's face. Now I almost had a baby. And when I went back to the little house, I could play with my own little brother.

"Thank you, Nancy," I said.

Oh Baby!

Babies are a lot of work, but they are gigundo fun, too! If you like babies, you'll *love* these fun facts, puzzles, and crafts all about babies. But don't cry. These activities aren't babyish. They're just goo-goo-goo-good fun!

Gigundo Fun Puzzles!

Hey, Baby Face, here come the puzzles!
You can check the answers to these puzzles on pages 136-138.

Oh Baby Wordsearch

For such tiny people, babies sure need a lot of stuff! How many words about babies can you find in this puzzle? The words go up, down, sideways, backwards, and diagonally. Look for: CRY, BLANKET, BOTTLE, CRIB, MOBILE, BOOTIES, DIAPER, TINY, WIPE, STROLLER, RATTLE, BOOK, HUG

```
C M D I A P E R G A
I O K Y U R E U S S
E B O N K L H W N E
L I O I T C R I B I
T L B T V R C P E T
T E O L Y Y N E A O
A B L A N K E T R O
R E L L O R T S A B
```

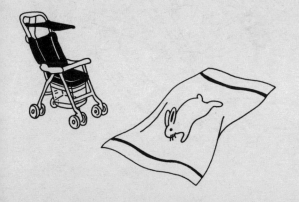

BABY WIPES

Daniel's Room

The Three Musketeers picked out the *cutest* stuff
for Daniel's room — all teddy bears and balloons.
There are 12 teddy bears hiding in this picture.
Find them all.

So Many Babies!

Karen was being silly when she wished Nancy's mom would have five babies all at once! She knew she would not have quintuplets. But there *are* five identical quintuplets in this picture. Which baby is not the same as the others?

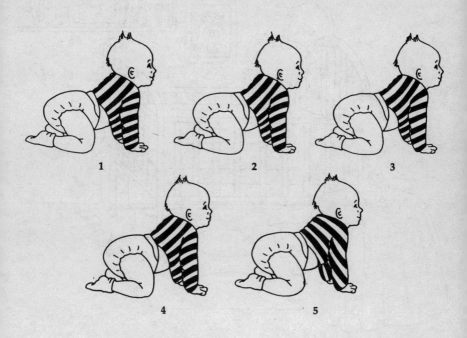

1

2

3

4

5

Nursery Nuthouse!

Whoops! Somebody has sent the wrong order to Nancy's house. A lot of these things are way too old for babies! Circle the things which don't belong in a nursery.

Babytalk Crossword Puzzle

Every time the phone rang, Karen and Nancy were sure the baby had been born. But it took awhile for Nancy's dad to call to say Nancy was officially a *big sister*! When grown-ups are waiting for an important call, they try to keep busy, by doing things like crossword puzzles. Here's a crossword puzzle for you to try while you are waiting for a special call.

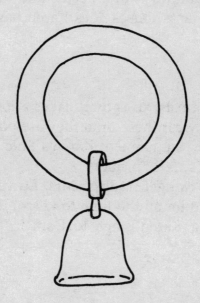

Across

1. Karen's big sister is named _____.
3. This is something Karen did to try and make a blanket for the new baby. Hint: She used two needles and red yarn.
4. Hyacynthia is Karen's baby _____.
6. When you blow up one of these it floats in the sky.
7. These went in groups of two on Noah's ark.
8. With a little felt and a needle and thread, Karen made a bottle-_____ for Daniel.
9. What you do with a needle and thread.
11. How many houses does Karen have?

Down

2. A toy a baby uses that makes a lot of noise.
4. Babies wear these until they are potty-trained.
5. What is the name of Karen's little brother?
6. Teddy _____ picnic.
10. Daniel can get so dirty. Mrs. Dawes has to do this to him all the time to keep him clean.
11. A song Karen sings to Daniel: "I'm a little _____."

112

Welcome Home, Daniel!

As far as Karen was concerned, it seemed like forever until Daniel came home from the hospital! What a Giant Slowpoke! Help Daniel find his way to his new home. Follow the maze.

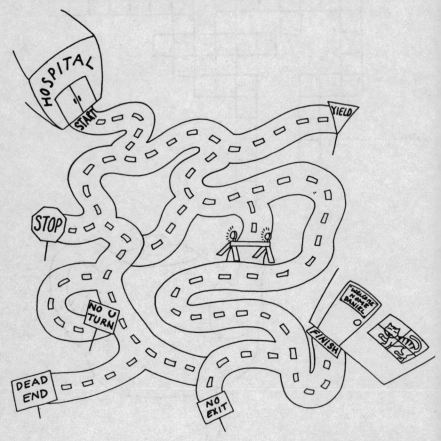

Baby Giggles

Here is Karen's new baby joke. It is super gigun-doly funny!
When Daniel cries, who wakes up?
Use the code to find the answer to Karen's joke.

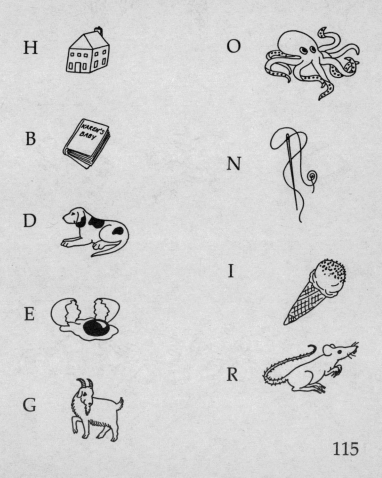

The whole

_____ _____ _____ _____ _____ —

_____ _____ _____ —

_____ _____ _____

Welcome to the Nursery!

Creative crafts to make

Baby nurseries are always filled with toys. Store-bought toys are fine, but nothing beats a hand-made gift. You probably don't want to make a bottle-warmer (Karen made enough of those for everyone!), but here are some fun baby toys you can make yourself.

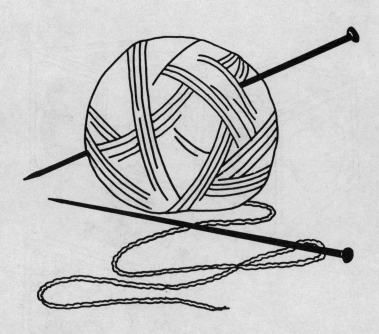

Big Blocks

You can make pretty counting blocks for a baby.

You will need:

three cube-shaped cardboard boxes
felt (many colors)
scissors
glue
pencil

Here's what you do:

1. Glue the lid of each box shut.
2. Cut six squares of felt. Make sure each square is large enough to cover a side of the box.
3. Glue the felt squares onto the box.
4. Cut out a number "1" from a piece of felt that is a different color from the felt you used to cover the block.
5. Glue the "1" to one side of the block.
6. Draw an apple onto a red piece of felt. Cut out the apple and glue it to another side of the block.
7. Repeat the steps above for the second block using the number "2" and two different shapes in place of the number "1" and the apple.
8. Repeat again, this time using a number "3" and three shapes.

Two by Two

While you have your glue and felt handy, why not try making this Noah's Ark picture? It's just like the one on Daniel's mezuzah.

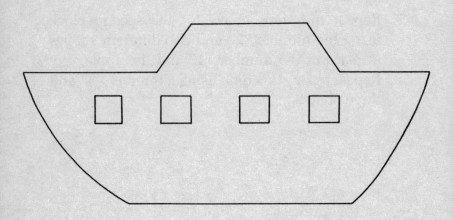

You will need:

felt (many colors)
posterboard
scissors
glue
patterns (the ones in this book or ones you draw yourself)
sparkles
markers

Here's what you do:

1. Cut the posterboard to the size you want your picture to be.
2. Cover the posterboard with felt. This will be your background.
3. Copy the pattern for the ark on page 120 on to a different piece of felt. Cut out the ark.
4. Glue your ark to the posterboard.
5. Trace each animal on the pattern page onto your felt. Be sure to trace each animal twice. Cut out all the animals.
6. Glue the animals to your picture.
7. Decorate your picture with sparkles, and markers.

Learning Your ABC's

Babies love to look at pictures. And with this easy-
to-make alphabet book, your favorite baby can
learn her ABC's, too!

You will need:

14 pieces of oaktag
ribbon
glue
holepunch
magazines
scissors
markers

Here's what you do:

1. Have a grown-up punch a hole in the upper left hand corner of each sheet of oaktag.
2. Tie the ribbon through the holes so that all the pages are fastened together.
3. With your marker, write *My First Book of ABC's* on the first page. This is the cover of your book. (You may want to write the baby's name here, too.)
4. On the next page, print a big letter A. Now look through magazines, cutting out pictures of "A" words. Cut out apples, airplanes, alligators, or anything else you can find. It helps to look for large-size pictures, since babies can't focus well on small things.
5. Glue the pictures to your "A" page.
6. On the next page, write the letter "B" and cut out all sorts of pictures of things that begin with the letter "B". Glue them to your "B" page.
7. Keep going until you have completed a page for every letter of the alphabet.

Make-Your-Own-Mobile

Here's how to make a black and white mobile. That's the kind babies *like* best because in the beginning, black and white are the colors babies *see* best.

(Remember, never hang anything in reach of a baby. Ask a grown-up to hang your mobile in a place where the baby can see it but not get to it. The mobiles that you buy in the store are specially made and tested so that they will be safe for a baby.)

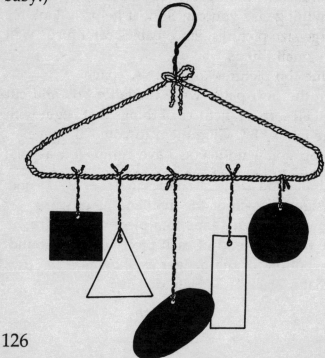

You will need:

a metal hanger
five lengths of black or white yarn
a ball of black yarn
black felt
white felt
glue
scissors

Here's what you do:

1. Wrap the yarn from the ball around and around the hanger until the entire hanger is covered with black yarn. Knot the yarn at the top when you are finished. Cut the yarn loose from the rest of the ball.
2. Cut out five pairs of shapes from the felt. Try a black circle and a white circle, a black square and a white square, a black triangle and a white triangle, and any other shapes you can think of. Glue the identical shapes together. Make one design for each of the five lengths of yarn.
3. Now glue each shape to a piece of cut yarn.
4. Tie the loose end of each piece of yarn around the bottom of the hanger as shown.
What a black and white delight!

Meet the Family

A friendly faces poster to make!
Babies love to look at faces. And what better faces to show a baby than the faces of the people who love her the most! So gather up some of the best shots of baby's mommy, daddy, sisters, brothers, and grandparents to make a very special poster you can hang in the baby's room. (Don't forget to ask permission to use the pictures before you get started.)

To make this poster you will also need scissors, glue, and posterboard.

Here's all you do:

1. Draw a large, simple shape on the poster board. A big star or a giant heart will work just fine.
2. Now arrange the photos so that they fill in the space inside your star or heart. Don't do any cutting or gluing until you've decided exactly where you want your pictures to go.
3. Now, carefully glue the pictures to the poster-board. You can cut away the backgrounds on some of the photos so that they will fit better.
4. When the poster is finished and dry, ask a grown-up to hang it on the baby's wall.
5. Whenever you get the chance, tell the baby the names of the people in the pictures. That's the way babies learn. One day, before you know it, the baby will put a pudgy finger on your picture and smile right at you!

Playing with Baby!

Games Babies Play

Babies learn from playing. When Karen and Nancy play peek-a-boo with Daniel, he's learning that people and things don't go away just because he can't see them. Baby animals also learn from the games they play.

Cheetah cubs play tag. Playing tag teaches them to run fast. When they get older, they'll have to run to catch food.

Young foxes play hide-and-seek. That's how they learn to sneak up on other animals when they are hunting for food.

Bear cubs love to wrestle. Wrestling for fun helps them grow strong enough to fight their enemies in the wild.

It's Rhyme Time!

Even nursery rhymes don't seem silly when you're saying them to a baby! Nancy's mom has told her that she sang nursery rhymes to Nancy when she was a baby. But it's been a long time since the Three Musketeers were babies. Here are some of the rhymes Nancy, Karen, and Hannie read to Daniel. Try them on a baby you know. It won't be long before that baby will be smiling a great big toothless grin!

Patty Cake

Patty cake
Patty cake
Baker's man
Bake me a cake as fast as you can!
Mix it in a bowl
Mark it with a B
And put it in the oven for Baby and me!

Peek-a-Boo

Peek-a-boo
I see you
I can see your dimples, too!

And here's one that will tickle any baby's funny bone. Remember, when you tickle a teeny tiny baby, you have to be extra careful!
To start, hold up one of the baby's feet. As you say each line, grab one of the baby's toes. When you get to the last line, tickle, tickle, tickle that baby all over!

This Little Piggy

This little piggy went to market
This little piggy stayed home
This little piggy had roast beef
This little piggy had none
And this little piggy . . .
Ran whee whee whee
All the way home!

What's in a Name?

Karen has a list of her favorite names all ready to
go, just in case one of her families decides to make
her gigundoly happy and have a new baby. Here
are some other name lists. These are the top ten
names for girls and boys in the United States for
the years 1950, 1980, and 1988. Are any of them
your favorites?

1950

Girls
Linda, Mary, Patricia, Susan, Deborah, Kathleen,
Barbara, Nancy, Carol, Sharon
Boys
Robert, James, Michael, John, David, William, Joseph, Thomas, Richard, Stephen

1980

Girls
Jennifer, Jessica, Melissa, Nicole, Stephanie, Christina, Tiffany, Michelle, Elizabeth, Lauren
Boys
Michael, Christopher, Jason, David, Brian, James, Robert, Matthew, Joseph, John

1988

Girls
Jessica, Jennifer, Stephanie, Melissa, Nicole, Ashley, Tiffany, Amanda, Christina, Samantha
Boys
Michael, Christopher, Jonathan, Daniel, Anthony, David, Joseph, Matthew, John, Andrew

Baby Books

Is your family expecting a new baby? Well, even if they're not, you'll get a real laugh when you read some of these books about new babies and their wacky families!

Babar's Little Girl by Laurent de Brunhoff

A Baby Sister for Frances by Russell Hoban

Betsy's Little Star by Carolyn Heywood

Nobody Asked Me if I Wanted a Baby Sister by Martha Alexander

Superfudge by Judy Blume

Answers

Oh Baby Wordsearch

```
C M D I A P E R G A
I O K Y U R E U S S
E B O N K L H W N E
L I O I T C R I B I
T L B T V R C P E T
T E O L Y Y N E A O
A B L A N K E T R O
R E L L O R T S A B
```

Daniel's Room

So Many Babies!

Number five is different.

Nursery Nuthouse!

Babytalk Crossword Puzzle

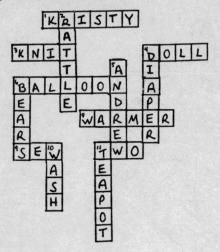

Welcome Home, Daniel!

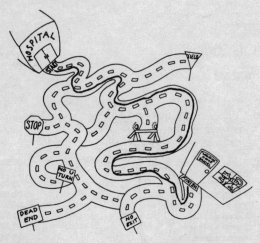

Baby Giggles
neighborhood

LITTLE ❤ APPLE ®

BABY SITTERS
Little Sister ™

by Ann M. Martin,
author of The Baby-sitters Club ®

More Titles... ➡

The Baby-sitters Little Sister titles continued...

Available wherever you buy books, or use this order form.

- -

Scholastic Inc., P.O. Box 7502, 2931 E. McCarty Street, Jefferson City, MO 65102

Please send me the books I have checked above. I am enclosing $ _____
(please add $2.00 to cover shipping and handling). Send check or money order – no
cash or C.O.Ds please.

Name _____ Birthdate _____

Address _____

City _____ State/Zip _____

Please allow four to six weeks for delivery. Offer good in U.S.A. only. Sorry, mail orders are not
available to residents to Canada. Prices subject to change.

BLS995